BERKLEY/FIRST PUBLISHING

CLASSICS ILLUSTRATED ™

EDGAR ALLAN POE

The Fall of the House of USHER

adapted by

P. CRAIG RUSSELL

script, layout artist

JAY GELDHOF

artist

WILLIE SCHUBERT
letterer

STEVE OLIFF and OLYOPTICS
color artist

A masterpiece of horror, Edgar Allan Poe's **The Fall of the House of Usher** delves the dark depths of the subconscious and traces the hidden terrors of the human soul. Never before and rarely since has a writer captured so completely the melancholy, the torment, and the passion that is embodied in a decadent and morbid state of mind. With his contemporary, Nathaniel Hawthorne, Poe was a founder of the American Gothic literary movement that blossomed before the Civil War. Poe used his own tortured life as an inspiration for his writing, the first volumes of which appeared in 1831. **The Fall of the House of Usher**, which reflected his obsession with death, first appeared in 1839 in *Burton's Gentleman's Magazine,* where Poe worked as co-editor; it was reprinted in 1840 in Poe's first short-story collection, *Tales of the Grotesque and Arabesque.* In 1844, following bouts with poverty, alcoholism, and romantic and professional failures, he produced the eerie poem *The Raven* for the New York *Evening News.* The popularity of that poem briefly propelled Poe into the literary spotlight. For the most part, though, he was criticized, demeaned, and condemned as a lunatic and literary fake: "the jingle man," Ralph Waldo Emerson huffed, dismissing Poe's works as all style and little substance. Only after his death was Poe recognized as a stylistic innovator and a master of language and narrative. Later reassessments — led by the French poets Baudelaire and Mallarmé — lauded Poe for his consistent command of mood, emotion and atmosphere; he was, judged William Yeats, "always and for all lands a great lyric poet." Not only are his poems and tales among the world's best-loved and most widely read, but they have influenced several generations of writers. Haunting, beautiful, full of rhythm and melody, Poe's forms, techniques, and theories inspired the post-Civil War American Bohemian writers, the French Symbolists, and were also later echoed in the works of such writers as T.S. Eliot and William Faulkner.

The Fall of the House of Usher
Classics Illustrated, Number 14

Wade Roberts, Editorial Director
Alex Wald, Art Director
Mike McCormick, Production Manager

PRINTING HISTORY
1st edition published September 1990

For information, address: First Publishing, Inc., 435 North LaSalle St., Chicago, Illinois 60610.

ISBN 0-425-12140-2

Distributed by Berkley Sales & Marketing, a division of The Berkley Publishing Group, 200 Madison Avenue, New York, New York 10016.

Printed in the United States of America
1 2 3 4 5 6 7 8 9 0

URING THE WHOLE OF A DULL, DARK, AND SOUNDLESS DAY IN THE AUTUMN OF THE YEAR, WHEN THE CLOUDS HUNG OPPRESSIVELY LOW IN THE HEAVENS, I HAD BEEN PASSING, ALONE ON HORSEBACK, THROUGH A SINGULARLY DREARY TRACT OF COUNTRY.

AT LENGTH, I FOUND MYSELF, AS THE SHADES OF THE EVENING DREW ON, WITHIN VIEW OF THE MELANCHOLY HOUSE OF USHER.

WITH THE FIRST GLIMPSE OF THE BUILDING, A SENSE OF INSUFFERABLE GLOOM PERVADED MY SPIRIT.

I LOOKED UPON THE VACANT EYE-LIKE WINDOWS WITH AN UTTER DEPRESSION OF SOUL WHICH I CAN COMPARE TO NO EARTHLY SENSATION MORE PROPERLY THAN TO THE AFTER-DREAM OF THE REVELLER UPON OPIUM--THE BITTER LAPSE INTO EVERYDAY LIFE--THE HIDEOUS DROPPING OFF OF THE VEIL.

THERE WAS AN ICINESS, A SINKING, A SICKENING OF THE HEART--AN UNREDEEMED DREARINESS OF THOUGHT WHICH NO GOADING OF THE IMAGINATION COULD TORTURE INTO AUGHT OF THE SUBLIME.

WHAT WAS IT THAT SO UNNERVED ME IN THE CONTEMPLATION OF THE HOUSE OF USHER?

I REINED MY HORSE TO THE BRINK OF A BLACK AND LURID TARN, AND GAZED DOWN WITH A SHUDDER UPON THE REMODELLED AND INVERTED IMAGES OF THE GREY SEDGE, AND THE GHASTLY TREE-STEMS, AND THE VACANT AND EYE-LIKE WINDOWS.

NEVERTHELESS, IN THIS MANSION OF GLOOM I NOW PROPOSED A SOJOURN OF SOME WEEKS. ITS PROPRIETOR, RODERICK USHER, HAD BEEN ONE OF MY BOYHOOD COMPANIONS. A LETTER FROM HIM HAD LATELY REACHED ME-- A LETTER WHICH, WITH ITS NERVOUS AGITATION, ALLOWED ME NO ROOM FOR HESITATION. I OBEYED FORTHWITH WHAT I CONSIDERED A VERY SINGULAR SUMMONS.

ALTHOUGH, AS BOYS, WE HAD BEEN INTIMATE ASSOCIATES, YET I REALLY KNEW LITTLE OF MY FRIEND.

I WAS AWARE, HOWEVER, THAT HIS VERY ANCIENT FAMILY HAD BEEN NOTED FOR A PECULIAR SENSITIVITY OF TEMPERAMENT, DISPLAYING ITSELF IN MANY WORKS OF EXALTED ART, AS WELL AS IN A PASSIONATE DEVOTION TO THE INTRICACIES OF MUSICAL SCIENCE.

AND IT MIGHT HAVE BEEN FOR THIS REASON ONLY THAT, WHEN I AGAIN UPLIFTED MY EYES TO THE HOUSE ITSELF, THERE GREW IN MY MIND A FANCY SO RIDICULOUS THAT I BUT MENTION IT TO SHOW THE VIVID FORCE OF THE SENSATIONS WHICH OPPRESSED ME.

I HAD LEARNED, TOO, THAT THE STEM OF THE USHER RACE HAD PUT FORTH, AT NO PERIOD, ANY ENDURING BRANCH; THAT THE ENTIRE FAMILY LAY IN THE DIRECT LINE OF DESCENT.

BECAUSE OF THIS, ALONG WITH THE CHARACTER, OF THE PREMISES, THE ORIGINAL TITLE OF THE ESTATE--HOUSE OF USHER--HAD COME IN THE MINDS OF THE PEASANTS TO DESCRIBE BOTH THE FAMILY AND THE MANSION.

I IMAGINED THAT ABOUT THE WHOLE MANSION AND DOMAIN THERE HUNG AN ATMOSPHERE WHICH HAD REEKED UP FROM THE DECAYED TREES, AND THE GREY WALL, AND THE SILENT TARN--A PESTILENT AND MYSTIC VAPOR.

PERHAPS THE EYE OF A SCRUTINIZING OBSERVER MIGHT HAVE DISCOVERED A BARELY PERCEPTIBLE FISSURE, WHICH, EXTENDING FROM THE ROOF, MADE ITS WAY DOWN THE WALL IN A ZIGZAG DIRECTION, UNTIL IT BECAME LOST IN THE SULLEN WATERS OF THE TARN.

NOTICING THESE THINGS, I RODE OVER A SHORT CAUSEWAY TO THE HOUSE.

SHAKING OFF WHAT MUST HAVE BEEN A DREAM, I SCANNED THE REAL ASPECT OF THE BUILDING. ITS PRINCIPAL FEATURE SEEMED TO BE AN EXCESSIVE ANTIQUITY. THE DISCOLORATION OF AGES HAD BEEN GREAT. MINUTE FUNGI HUNG IN A FINE TANGLED WEB-WORK FROM THE EAVES. BEYOND THIS, HOWEVER, THE FABRIC GAVE LITTLE TOKEN OF INSTABILITY.

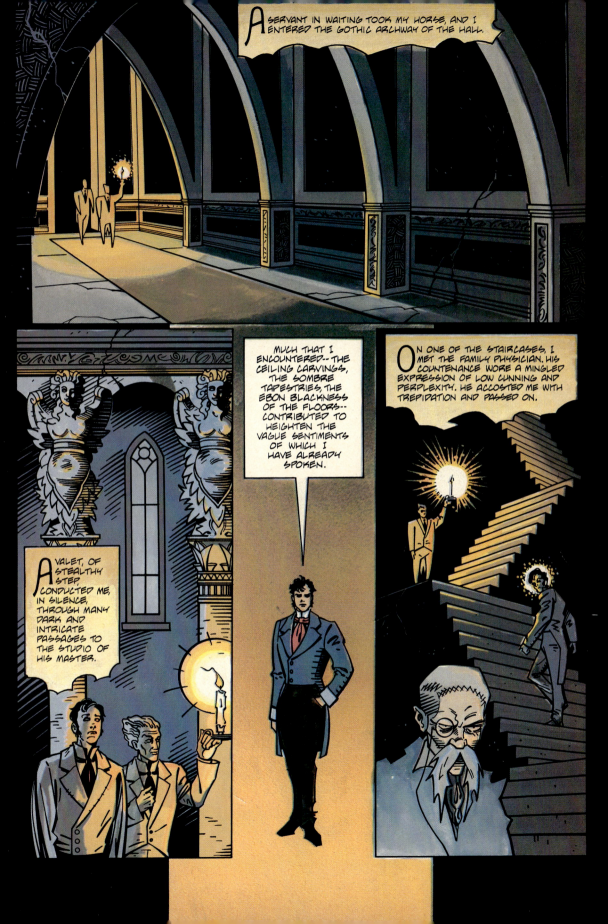

A SERVANT IN WAITING TOOK MY HORSE, AND I ENTERED THE GOTHIC ARCHWAY OF THE HALL.

MUCH THAT I ENCOUNTERED-- THE CEILING CARVINGS, THE SOMBRE TAPESTRIES, THE EBON BLACKNESS OF THE FLOORS-- CONTRIBUTED TO HEIGHTEN THE VAGUE SENTIMENTS OF WHICH I HAVE ALREADY SPOKEN.

ON ONE OF THE STAIRCASES, I MET THE FAMILY PHYSICIAN. HIS COUNTENANCE WORE A MINGLED EXPRESSION OF LOW CUNNING AND PERPLEXITY. HE ACCOSTED ME WITH TREPIDATION AND PASSED ON.

A VALET, OF STEALTHY STEP, CONDUCTED ME, IN SILENCE, THROUGH MANY DARK AND INTRICATE PASSAGES TO THE STUDIO OF HIS MASTER.

THE VALET THREW OPEN A DOOR AND USHERED ME INTO THE PRESENCE OF HIS MASTER.

THE ROOM IN WHICH I FOUND MYSELF WAS VERY LARGE AND LOFTY. THE EYE STRUGGLED IN VAIN TO REACH THE REMOTER ANGLES OF THE CHAMBER, OR THE RECESSES OF THE VAULTED AND FRETTED CEILING.

I FELT THAT I BREATHED AN ATMOSPHERE OF SORROW; AN AIR OF STERN, DEEP, AND IRREDEEMABLE GLOOM.

UPON MY ENTRANCE, USHER AROSE FROM A SOFA ON WHICH HE HAD BEEN LYING...

...AND GREETED ME WITH A VIVACIOUS WARMTH WHICH HAD MUCH IN IT, I AT FIRST THOUGHT, OF AN OVERDONE CORDIALITY.

A GLANCE, HOWEVER, AT HIS COUNTENANCE, CONVINCED ME OF HIS PERFECT SINCERITY.

FOR SOME MOMENTS, I GAZED UPON HIM WITH A FEELING HALF OF PITY, HALF OF AWE. IT WAS WITH DIFFICULTY THAT I COULD BRING MYSELF TO ADMIT THAT THE WAN BEING BEFORE ME WAS THE COMPANION OF MY BOYHOOD.

YET THE CHARACTER OF HIS FACE HAD BEEN AT ALL TIMES REMARKABLE. A CADAVEROUSNESS OF COMPLEXION; EYES LARGE AND LUMINOUS; LIPS SOMEWHAT THIN AND PALLID; HAIR OF A WEB-LIKE SOFTNESS; THESE FEATURES MADE UP A COUNTENANCE NOT EASILY TO BE FORGOTTEN.

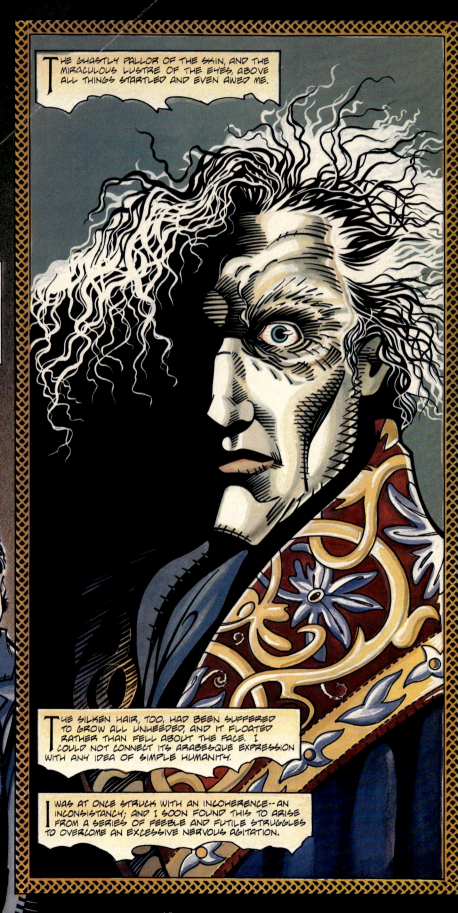

THE GHASTLY PALLOR OF THE SKIN, AND THE MIRACULOUS LUSTRE OF THE EYES, ABOVE ALL THINGS STARTLED AND EVEN AWED ME.

AND NOW IN THE EXAGGERATION OF THESE FEATURES LAY SO MUCH CHANGE, THAT I DOUBTED TO WHOM I SPOKE.

THE SILKEN HAIR, TOO, HAD BEEN SUFFERED TO GROW ALL UNHEEDED, AND IT FLOATED RATHER THAN FELL ABOUT THE FACE. I COULD NOT CONNECT ITS ARABESQUE EXPRESSION WITH ANY IDEA OF SIMPLE HUMANITY.

I WAS AT ONCE STRUCK WITH AN INCOHERENCE—AN INCONSISTANCY; AND I SOON FOUND THIS TO ARISE FROM A SERIES OF FEEBLE AND FUTILE STRUGGLES TO OVERCOME AN EXCESSIVE NERVOUS AGITATION.

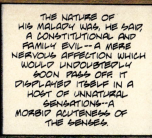 THE NATURE OF HIS MALADY WAS, HE SAID, A CONSTITUTIONAL AND FAMILY EVIL--A MERE NERVOUS AFFECTION WHICH WOULD UNDOUBTEDLY SOON PASS OFF. IT DISPLAYED ITSELF IN A HOST OF UNNATURAL SENSATIONS--A MORBID ACUTENESS OF THE SENSES.

ONLY THE MOST INSIPID FOOD WAS ENDURABLE;

HE COULD WEAR ONLY GARMENTS OF A CERTAIN TEXTURE;

THE ODORS OF ALL FLOWERS WERE OPPRESSIVE;

HIS EYES WERE TORTURED BY EVEN A FAINT LIGHT;

AND THERE WERE ONLY PECULIAR SOUNDS--FROM STRINGED INSTRUMENTS-- WHICH DID NOT INSPIRE HIM WITH HORROR.

I LEARNED, MOREOVER, THROUGH BROKEN AND EQUIVOCAL HINTS, ANOTHER SINGULAR FEATURE OF HIS MENTAL CONDITION.

HE WAS ENCHAINED BY CERTAIN SUPERSTITIOUS IMPRESSIONS IN REGARD TO THE DWELLING WHICH HE TENANTED...

IN REGARD TO AN INFLUENCE WHOSE FORCE WAS CONVEYED IN TERMS TOO SHADOWY HERE TO BE RESTATED...

AN INFLUENCE WHICH SOME PECULIARITIES IN THE FORM AND SUBSTANCE OF HIS FAMILY MANSION HAD OBTAINED OVER HIS SPIRIT...

AN EFFECT WHICH THE PHYSIQUE OF THE GREY WALLS AND TURRETS, HAD, AT LENGTH, BROUGHT ABOUT UPON THE MORALE OF HIS EXISTENCE.

IN THIS UNNERVED--IN THIS PITIABLE CONDITION--I FEEL THAT THE PERIOD WILL SOONER OR LATER ARRIVE WHEN I MUST ABANDON LIFE AND REASON TOGETHER...

...IN SOME STRUGGLE WITH THE GRIM PHANTASM...

FEAR.

I REGARDED HER WITH AN UTTER ASTONISHMENT NOT UNMINGLED WITH DREAD--AND YET I FOUND IT IMPOSSIBLE TO ACCOUNT FOR SUCH FEELINGS.

HE ADMITTED THAT MUCH OF HIS PECULIAR GLOOM COULD BE TRACED TO A MORE NATURAL AND FAR MORE PALPABLE ORIGIN-- TO THE SEVERE AND LONG ILLNESS OF A TENDERLY BELOVED SISTER-- HIS SOLE COMPANION FOR LONG YEARS--HIS LAST AND ONLY RELATIVE ON EARTH.

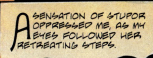

A SENSATION OF STUPOR OPPRESSED ME, AS MY EYES FOLLOWED HER RETREATING STEPS.

HER DECEASE WILL LEAVE ME THE LAST OF THE ANCIENT RACE OF THE USHERS.

THE DISEASE OF THE LADY MADELINE HAD LONG BAFFLED THE SKILL OF HER PHYSICIANS.

A SETTLED APATHY, A GRADUAL WASTING AWAY, AND THE FREQUENT ALTHOUGH TRANSIENT AFFECTIONS OF A PARTIALLY CATALEPTICAL CHARACTER, WERE THE UNUSUAL DIAGNOSIS.

HITHERTO SHE HAD STEADILY BORNE UP AGAINST THE PRESSURE OF HER MALADY...

...BUT ON THE EVENING OF MY ARRIVAL, SHE SUCCUMBED TO THE PROSTRATING POWER OF THE DESTROYER...

...AND I LEARNED THAT THE GLIMPSE I HAD OBTAINED WOULD THUS PROBABLY BE THE LAST I SHOULD OBTAIN--THAT THE LADY, AT LEAST WHILE LIVING, WOULD BE SEEN BY ME NO MORE.

FOR SEVERAL DAYS, HER NAME WAS UNMENTIONED BY EITHER USHER OR MYSELF, AS I ENDEAVORED TO ALLEVIATE THE MELANCHOLY OF MY FRIEND.

WE PAINTED AND READ TOGETHER; OR I LISTENED, AS IF IN A DREAM, TO THE WILD IMPROVISATIONS OF HIS SPEAKING GUITAR.

I CAME TO PERCEIVE THE FUTILITY OF ALL ATTEMPT AT CHEERING A MIND FROM WHICH DARKNESS POURED FORTH UPON ALL OBJECTS OF THE MORTAL AND PHYSICAL UNIVERSE, IN ONE UNCEASING RADIATION OF GLOOM.

FROM THE PAINTINGS OVER WHICH HIS ELABORATE FANCY BROODED, I WOULD IN VAIN ENDEAVOR TO EDUCE THAT WHICH COULD BE EXPLAINED BY MERE WORDS-- THE SHADOW WHICH I FELT IN HIS CONTEMPLATION OF THE GLOWING, YET CONCRETE, REVERIES OF THE PAINTER FUSELI.

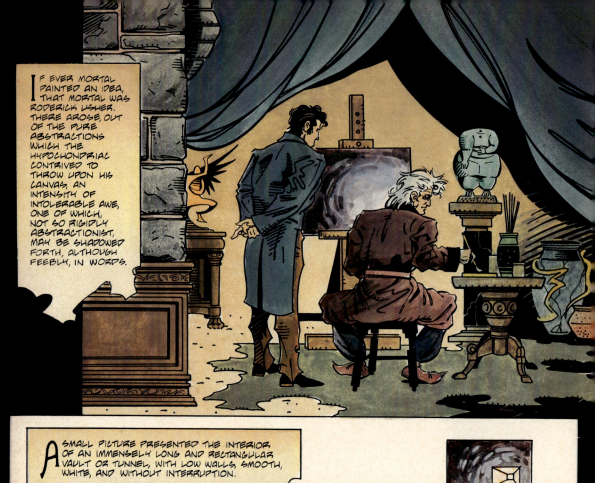

If ever mortal painted an idea, that mortal was Roderick Usher. There arose, out of the pure abstractions which the hypochondriac contrived to throw upon his canvas, an intensity of intolerable awe, one of which, not so rigidly abstractionist, may be shadowed forth, although feebly, in words.

A small picture presented the interior of an immensely long and rectangular vault or tunnel, with low walls, smooth, white, and without interruption.

Certain points of the design conveyed the idea that this excavation lay at an exceeding depth below the earth's surface.

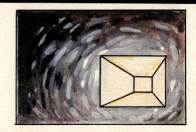

No outlet was observed, no torch or other source of light was discernable, yet a flood of intense rays bathed the whole in a ghastly and inappropriate splendor.

I HAVE SPOKEN OF THAT MORBID AUDITORY CONDITION WHICH RENDERED MOST MUSIC INTOLERABLE TO THE SUFFERER.

IT WAS, PERHAPS, THE NARROW LIMITS TO WHICH HE CONFINED HIMSELF, UPON THE GUITAR, WHICH GAVE BIRTH TO THE FANTASTIC CHARACTER OF HIS PERFORMANCES.

BUT THE FERVID FACILITY OF HIS IMPROMPTUS COULD NOT BE ACCOUNTED FOR. THEY WERE, IN THE NOTES, AS WELL AS IN THE WORDS, THE RESULT OF THAT INTENSE MENTAL CONCENTRATION OBSERVABLE ONLY IN MOMENTS OF THE HIGHEST ARTIFICIAL EXCITEMENT.

THE WORDS OF ONE OF THESE RHAPSODIES I HAVE EASILY REMEMBERED, BECAUSE, I FANCIED THAT I PERCEIVED, FOR THE FIRST TIME, A FULL CONSCIOUSNESS ON THE PART OF USHER, OF THE TOTTERING OF HIS LOFTY REASON UPON HER THRONE.

In the greenest of our valleys,
    By good angels tenanted,
Once a fair and stately palace··
    Radiant palace··reared its head.
In the monarch Thought's dominion··
    It stood there!
Never seraph spread a pinion
    Over fabric half so fair.

Banners yellow, glorious, golden,
    On its roof did float and flow
(This··all this··was in the olden
    Time long ago);
And every gentle air that dallied,
    In that sweet day,
Along the ramparts plumed and pallid,
    A winged odour went away.

Wanderers in that happy valley
    Through two luminous windows saw
Spirits moving musically
    To a lute's well-tuned law,
Round about a throne, where sitting
    (Porphyrogene!)
In state his glory well befitting,
    The ruler of the realm was seen.

And all with pearl and ruby glowing
    Was the fair palace door,
Through which came flowing, flowing,
flowing
    And sparkling evermore,
A troop of echoes whose sweet duty
    Was but to sing,
In voices of surpassing beauty,
    The wit and wisdom of their king.

But evil things, in robes of sorrow,
    Assailed the monarch's high estate;
(Ah, let us mourn, for never morrow
    Shall dawn upon him, desolate!)
And, round about his home, the glory
    That blushed and bloomed
Is but a dim-remembered story
    Of the old time entombed.

And travellers now within that valley,
    Through the red-litten windows, see
Vast forms that move fantastically
    To a discordant melody;
While, like a rapid ghastly river,
    Through the pale door,
A hideous throng rush out forever,
    And laugh··but smile no more.

I WELL REMEMBER THAT SUGGESTIONS ARISING FROM THIS BALLAD LED US INTO A TRAIN OF THOUGHT WHEREIN THERE BECAME MANIFEST AN OPINION OF USHER'S, WHICH, IN ITS GENERAL FORM, WAS THAT OF THE SENTIENCE OF ALL VEGETABLE THINGS. IN HIS DISORDERED FANCY, THE IDEA HAD ASSUMED A MORE DARING CHARACTER, AND TRESPASSED UPON THE KINGDOM OF INORGANIZATION.

THE BELIEF WAS CONNECTED WITH THE GREY STONES OF THE HOME OF HIS FOREFATHERS. THE CONDITIONS OF THE SENTIENCE HAD BEEN THERE, HE IMAGINED, IN THE ORDER OF THEIR ARRANGEMENT, IN THE MANY FUNGI WHICH OVERSPREAD THEM, AND OF THE DECAYED TREES WHICH STOOD AROUND--ABOVE ALL, IN THE LONG UNDISTURBED ENDURANCE OF THIS ARRANGEMENT, AND IN ITS REDUPLICATION IN THE STILL WATERS OF THE TARN.

ITS EVIDENCE WAS TO BE SEEN, HE SAID, IN THE GRADUAL YET CERTAIN CONDENSATION OF AN ATMOSPHERE OF THEIR OWN ABOUT THE WATERS AND THE WALLS.

THE RESULT WAS DISCOVERABLE, HE ADDED, IN THAT SILENT AND TERRIBLE INFLUENCE WHICH FOR CENTURIES HAD MOLDED THE DESTINIES OF HIS FAMILY...

...AND MADE HIM WHAT I NOW SAW HIM--WHAT HE WAS.

OUR BOOKS--THE BOOKS WHICH, FOR YEARS, HAD FORMED NO SMALL PORTION OF THE MENTAL EXISTENCE OF THE INVALID--WERE, AS MIGHT BE SUPPOSED, IN STRICT KEEPING WITH THIS CHARACTER OF PHANTASM.

WE PORED OVER SUCH WORKS AS THE BELPHEGOR OF MACHIAVELLI...

...THE SUBTERRANEAN VOYAGE OF NICHOLAS KLIMM BY HOLBERG...

...AND THE HEAVEN AND HELL OF SWEDENBORG.

HIS CHIEF DELIGHT, HOWEVER, WAS TO BE FOUND IN THE PERUSAL OF AN EXCEEDINGLY RARE AND CURIOUS BOOK IN QUARTO GOTHIC--THE MANUAL OF A FORGOTTEN CHURCH--THE VIGILAE MORTUORUM SECUNDUM CHORUM ECCLESIAE MAGUNTINAE.

I COULD NOT HELP THINKING OF THE WILD RITUAL OF THIS WORK, AND OF ITS PROBABLE INFLUENCE UPON THE HYPOCHONDRIAC, WHEN ONE EVENING, HAVING INFORMED ME ABRUPTLY THAT THE LADY MADELINE WAS NO MORE, HE STATED HIS INTENTION OF PRESERVING HER CORPSE FOR A FORTNIGHT--BEFORE ITS FINAL INTERMENT--IN ONE OF THE BUILDING'S NUMEROUS VAULTS.

THE BROTHER HAD BEEN LED TO HIS RESOLUTION (SO HE TOLD ME) BY CONSIDERATION OF THE UNUSUAL CHARACTER OF THE MALADY OF THE DECEASED, OF CERTAIN OBTRUSIVE AND EAGER INQUIRIES ON THE PART OF HER MEDICAL MEN...

...AND OF THE REMOTE AND EXPOSED SITUATION OF THE BURIAL GROUND OF THE FAMILY.

I WILL NOT DENY THAT, WHEN I CALLED TO MIND THE SINISTER COUNTENANCE OF THE PERSON WHOM I MET UPON THE STAIRCASE ON THE DAY OF MY ARRIVAL, I HAD NO DESIRE TO OPPOSE WHAT I REGARDED AS AT BEST A HARMLESS, AND BY NO MEANS AN UNNATURAL, PRECAUTION.

AT USHER'S REQUEST, I AIDED HIM IN THE ARRANGEMENTS FOR THE TEMPORARY ENTOMBMENT. THE BODY HAVING BEEN ENCOFFINED, WE TWO ALONE BORE IT TO ITS REST.

THE VAULT IN WHICH WE PLACED IT WAS SMALL, DAMP, AND, ENTIRELY WITHOUT MEANS OF ADMISSION FOR LIGHT; LYING AT GREAT DEPTH, IMMEDIATELY BENEATH THAT PORTION OF THE BUILDING IN WHICH WAS MY OWN SLEEPING APARTMENT.

IT HAD BEEN USED, APPARENTLY, IN REMOTE TIMES, FOR THE WORST PURPOSE OF A DUNGEON, AND, IN LATER DAYS, AS A PLACE OF DEPOSIT FOR GUNPOWDER, AS THE LONG ARCHWAY THROUGH WHICH WE REACHED IT, WAS CAREFULLY SHEATHED WITH COPPER.

THE DOOR, OF MASSIVE IRON, HAD BEEN, ALSO, SIMILARLY PROTECTED. ITS IMMENSE WEIGHT CAUSED AN UNUSUALLY SHARP, GRATING SOUND, AS IT MOVED UPON ITS HINGES.

HAVING DEPOSITED OUR MOURNFUL BURDEN UPON TRESTLES WITHIN THIS REGION OF HORROR, WE TURNED ASIDE THE YET UNSCREWED LID OF THE COFFIN AND LOOKED UPON THE FACE OF THE TENANT.

A STRIKING SIMILITUDE BETWEEN THE BROTHER AND SISTER NOW FIRST ARRESTED MY ATTENTION, AND FROM USHER I LEARNED THAT THE DECEASED AND HIMSELF HAD BEEN TWINS, AND THAT SYMPATHIES OF A SCARCELY INTELLIGIBLE NATURE HAD ALWAYS EXISTED BETWEEN THEM.

THE DISEASE WHICH HAD THUS ENTOMBED THE LADY IN THE MATURITY OF YOUTH, HAD LEFT, AS USUAL IN ALL MALADIES OF A STRICTLY CATALEPTICAL CHARACTER, THE MOCKERY OF A FAINT BLUSH UPON THE BOSOM AND THE FACE...

...AND THAT SUSPICIOUSLY LINGERING SMILE UPON THE LIP...

...WHICH IS SO TERRIBLE IN DEATH.

WE REPLACED AND SCREWED DOWN THE LID, AND, HAVING SECURED THE DOOR OF IRON, MADE OUR WAY, WITH TOIL, INTO THE SCARCELY LESS GLOOMY APARTMENTS OF THE UPPER PORTIONS OF THE HOUSE.

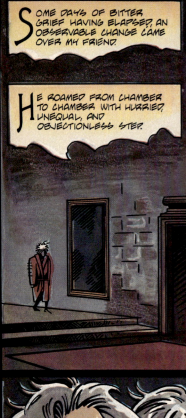

SOME DAYS OF BITTER GRIEF HAVING ELAPSED, AN OBSERVABLE CHANGE CAME OVER MY FRIEND.

HE ROAMED FROM CHAMBER TO CHAMBER WITH HURRIED, UNEQUAL, AND OBJECTIONLESS STEP.

HIS PALLOR HAD ASSUMED A MORE GHASTLY HUE-- BUT THE LUMINOUSNESS OF HIS EYE HAD UTTERLY GONE.

A TREMULOUS QUAVER, AS IF OF EXTREME TERROR, HABITUALLY CHARACTERIZED HIS UTTERANCE.

THERE WERE TIMES, I THOUGHT HIS UNCEASINGLY AGITATED MIND WAS LABORING WITH SOME OPPRESSIVE SECRET.

AT TIMES, AGAIN, I WAS OBLIGED TO RESOLVE ALL INTO THE INEXPLICABLE VAGARIES OF MADNESS, FOR I BEHELD HIM GAZING UPON VACANCY FOR LONG HOURS, IN THE PROFOUNDEST ATTENTION, AS IF LISTENING TO SOME IMAGINARY SOUND.

IT WAS NO WONDER THAT THIS CONDITION TERRIFIED--THAT IT INFECTED ME.

I FELT CREEPING UPON ME, BY SLOW YET CERTAIN DEGREES... THE WILD INFLUENCES OF HIS OWN FANTASTIC SUPERSTITIONS.

IT WAS, ESPECIALLY, UPON RETIRING TO BED LATE IN THE NIGHT OF THE SEVENTH OR EIGHTH DAY AFTER THE PLACING OF THE LADY MADELINE WITHIN THE DUNGEON, THAT I EXPERIENCED THE FULL POWER OF SUCH FEELINGS.

I ENDEAVORED TO BELIEVE THAT MUCH OF WHAT I FELT WAS DUE TO THE BUILDING INFLUENCE OF THE GLOOMY FURNITURE OF THE ROOM--OF THE DARK AND TATTERED DRAPERIES, WHICH SWAYED FITFULLY TO AND FRO UPON THE WALLS.

BUT MY EFFORTS WERE FRUITLESS.

GRADUALLY, THERE SAT UPON MY HEART AN INCUBUS OF UTTERLY CAUSELESS ALARM.

SHAKING THIS OFF WITH A GASP AND A STRUGGLE, I UPLIFTED MYSELF...

...AND, PEERING WITHIN THE INTENSE DARKNESS OF THE CHAMBER, HEARKENED--I KNOW NOT WHY--TO CERTAIN LOW AND INDEFINITE SOUNDS WHICH CAME THROUGH THE PAUSES OF THE STORM, I KNEW NOT WHENCE.

OVERPOWERED BY AN INTENSE SENTIMENT OF HORROR, I THREW ON MY CLOTHES AND ENDEAVORED TO AROUSE MYSELF FROM THE PITIABLE CONDITION INTO WHICH I HAD FALLEN.

I HAD TAKEN BUT FEW TURNS IN THIS MANNER, WHEN A LIGHT STEP ARRESTED MY ATTENTION. I RECOGNIZED IT AS THAT OF USHER. HE RAPPED, WITH A GENTLE TOUCH, AT MY DOOR, AND ENTERED, BEARING A LAMP.

THERE WAS A SPECIES OF MAD HILARITY IN HIS EYES-- A RESTRAINED HYSTERIA IN HIS WHOLE DEMEANOR.

AND YOU HAVE NOT SEEN IT? BUT, STAY! YOU SHALL!

HE HURRIED TO ONE OF THE CASEMENTS, AND THREW IT FREELY OPEN TO THE STORM.

THE IMPETUOUS FURY OF THE ENTERING GUST NEARLY LIFTED US FROM OUR FEET.

IT WAS, INDEED, A TEMPESTUOUS YET BEAUTIFUL NIGHT, SINGULAR IN ITS TERROR AND ITS BEAUTY. HUGE MASSES OF AGITATED VAPOR GLOWED IN THE UNNATURAL LIGHT OF A FAINTLY LUMINOUS, AND DISTINCTLY VISIBLE GASEOUS EXHALATION WHICH ENSHROUDED THE MANSION.

THE ANTIQUE VOLUME WAS THE MAD TRIST OF SIR LANCELOT CHANNING. I HAD ARRIVED AT THAT PORTION OF THE STORY WHERE ETHELRED, THE HERO, HAVING SOUGHT IN VAIN FOR PEACEABLE ADMISSION INTO THE HERMIT'S DWELLING, MAKES AN ENTRANCE BY FORCE.

...but Ethelred, now entering, was sore enraged and amazed to perceive no signal of the maliceful hermit; but in the stead thereof, a dragon of a scale and prodigious demeanor which sat in guard before a shield of shining brass.

Ethelred uplifted his mace, and struck upon the head of the dragon, which fell before him with a shriek so horrid and harsh, the like whereof was never before heard.

Here again I paused abruptly in wild amazement that I did actually hear a low and distant screaming or grating sound--the exact counterpart of what my fancy had already conjured up for the dragon's unnatural shriek.

32

OPPRESSED, AS I WAS, BY WONDER AND EXTREME TERROR, I RETAINED SUFFICIENT PRESENCE OF MIND TO AVOID EXCITING THE SENSITIVE NERVOUSNESS OF MY COMPANION; ALTHOUGH A STRANGE ALTERATION HAD TAKEN PLACE IN HIS DEMEANOR, AND HE ROCKED FROM SIDE TO SIDE WITH A CONSTANT AND UNIFORM SWAY.

AND NOW, THE CHAMPION, HAVING ESCAPED FROM THE TERRIBLE FURY OF THE DRAGON, APPROACHED TO WHERE THE SHIELD WAS UPON THE WALL; WHICH TARRIED NOT FOR HIS COMING, BUT FELL DOWN TO HIS FEET UPON THE SILVER FLOOR, WITH A MIGHTY GREAT AND TERRIBLE RINGING SOUND.

NO SOONER HAD THESE SYLLABLES PASSED MY LIPS, THAN I BECAME AWARE OF A DISTINCT, METALLIC, YET APPARENTLY MUFFLED REVERBERATION.

COMPLETELY UNNERVED, I LEAPED TO MY FEET, BUT THE MEASURED ROCKING MOVEMENT OF USHER WAS UNDISTURBED.

AS I PLACED MY HAND UPON HIS SHOULDER, THERE CAME A STRONG SHUDDER OVER HIS WHOLE PERSON; AND I SAW THAT HE SPOKE IN A LOW, HURRIED, AND GIBBERING MURMUR, AS IF UNCONSCIOUS OF MY PRESENCE.

BENDING CLOSELY OVER HIM, I AT LENGTH DRANK IN THE HIDEOUS IMPORT OF HIS WORDS.

AS IF THE SUPERHUMAN ENERGY OF HIS UTTERANCE HAD THE POTENCY OF A SPELL -- THE HUGE ANTIQUE PANELS TO WHICH THE SPEAKER POINTED, THREW SLOWLY BACK, UPON THE INSTANT, THEIR PONDEROUS AND HEAVY JAWS.

IT WAS THE WORK OF THE RUSHING GUST -- BUT THEN WITHOUT THOSE DOORS THERE *DID* STAND THE LOFTY AND ENSHROUDED FIGURE OF THE LADY MADELINE OF USHER, THE EVIDENCE OF SOME BITTER STRUGGLE UPON EVERY PORTION OF HER EMACIATED FRAME.

FOR A MOMENT SHE REMAINED TREMBLING AND REELING TO AND FRO UPON THE THRESHOLD...

...THEN, WITH A LOW MOANING CRY...

...FELL HEAVILY INWARD UPON THE PERSON OF HER BROTHER, AND IN HER VIOLENT AND NOW FINAL DEATH-AGONIES...

...BORE HIM TO THE FLOOR A CORPSE, AND A VICTIM TO THE TERRORS HE HAD ANTICIPATED.

ROM THAT CHAMBER, FROM THAT MANSION, I FLED AGHAST. THE STORM WAS STILL ABROAD IN ALL ITS WRATH AS I FOUND MYSELF CROSSING THE OLD CAUSEWAY.

SUDDENLY THERE SHOT ALONG THE PATH A WILD LIGHT, AND I TURNED TO SEE WHENCE A GLEAM SO UNUSUAL COULD HAVE ISSUED; FOR THE VAST HOUSE AND ITS SHADOWS WERE ALONE BEHIND ME.

THE RADIANCE WAS THAT OF THE FULL, SETTING, AND BLOOD-RED MOON WHICH NOW SHONE VIVIDLY THROUGH THAT ONCE BARELY DISCERNABLE FISSURE OF WHICH I HAVE BEFORE SPOKEN AS EXTENDING FROM THE ROOF OF THE BUILDING, IN A ZIG-ZAG DIRECTION TO THE BASE.

WHILE I GAZED THIS FISSURE RAPIDLY WIDENED--THERE CAME THE BREATH OF THE WHIRLWIND.

...THE ENTIRE ORB OF THE SATELLITE BURST AT ONCE UPON MY SIGHT...

...MY BRAIN REELED AS I SAW THE MIGHTY WALLS RUSHING ASUNDER...

...THERE WAS A LONG TUMULTUOUS SHOUTING SOUND LIKE THE VOICE OF A THOUSAND WATERS.

...AND THE DEEP AND DANK TARN AT MY FEET CLOSED SULLENLY AND SILENTLY...

...OVER THE FRAGMENTS OF THE "HOUSE OF USHER."

END

EDGAR ALLAN POE was born in Boston on January 19, 1809, the son of itinerant actors. Before he was three, Poe, his older brother and his younger sister were orphaned. They were taken in by John Allan, a Richmond, Virginia, merchant; never legally adopted, Poe employed his foster father's surname as his middle name. With the Allans, he spent five years (1815-1820) in England. After returning to Richmond, Poe attended a private school and then entered the University of Virginia at the age of 17. After accumulating heavy gambling debts, he withdrew less than a year later, fled to Boston and enlisted in the army. Anonymously and at his own expense, Poe published *Tamerlane,* his first poetry collection, in 1827. He entered West Point in 1830 following his discharge from the army, but was dismissed as a troublemaker the following year. Poe continued to write poems and short fiction, but labored unsuccessfully until *MS. Found in a Bottle* won a short-story contest and landed him a job with the *Southern Literary Messenger.* In 1836, Poe married his 14-year-old cousin, Virginia Clemm, and settled in Richmond with his new bride and her mother. They moved to New York in 1837, where Poe, supporting his family by taking hack writing jobs, published *The Narrative of Arthur Gordon Pym.* In 1838, the family moved to Philadelphia and Poe briefly served as co-editor of *Burton's Gentleman's Magazine,* to which he contributed *The Fall of the House of Usher,* and, later, as literary editor of *Graham's Magazine,* which published *The Masque of the Red Death* and other stories. *Tales of the Grotesque and Arabesque,* Poe's first short-story collection, appeared in 1840. During the next six years, Poe, briefly associated with several other periodicals, published a number of poems and stories, including *The Raven, The Pit and the Pendulum* and *The Cask of Amontillado.* Poe's wife died in 1847; in his grief, Poe embarked upon several disastrous love affairs, attempted suicide, and drank heavily. During his last two years, Poe's entire literary output consisted of four poems: *Eldorado, The Bells, Annabel Lee* and *Ulalume.* In 1849, travelling by train from Richmond to New York, Poe disappeared in Baltimore. Five days later, he was found delirious in the streets. Poe died less than a week later, on October 7, 1849, and was buried in Baltimore beside his wife.

JAY GELDHOF was born in Kent, Ohio, in 1960. He attended the Kubert School of Cartoon and Graphic Art in Dover, New Jersey. Geldhof first introduced his vibrant style in *Grendel,* and his credits also include *Epic Illustrated, Badger Goes Berserk,* and *Elvira's House of Mystery.* He would like to thank Jill Thompson and Troy Tinker.

P. CRAIG RUSSELL was born in Wellsville, Ohio, in 1951. He received an art degree from the University of Cincinnati. Russell is known for his graphic adaptations of operas, including Wagner's *Parsifal* and Mozart's *The Magic Flute.* His credits also include illustrations for Michael Moorcock's *Elric of Melniboné* and Rudyard Kipling's *The Jungle Books.* With artist Jill Thompson, Russell adapted Nathaniel Hawthorne's *The Scarlet Letter* for *Classics Illustrated.*